TIME DILEMMA

THE TIME TRAVEL PARADOX

SURYANSH TRIPATHI

Dedicating to my loving parents, who encouraged me to publish that awesomeness book with the world.

Welcome to 'The Time's Dilemma'! If you're fascinated by time travel, paradoxes, and thrilling adventures, this book is perfect for you. With no age restrictions, everyone can enjoy this captivating book with amazing adventures!

Join the journey of a boy and girl as they travel through time to save humanity and shape a brighter future for forthcoming generations.

Contents

Foreword

Myself is reviewer of this book and this book written about a future paradoxes that is related to time travel .

The genre of this book is fiction , so I am recommend this book to the age group like 8 to max because it contain mostly easy words that is suitable for a child.

Preface

The Time's Dilemma consists of the adventure , and time paradox scenes.

In this book , A teen aged boy named Robin and a teen aged girl like a 17 to 19 year old
girl will travel in the future to save humanity !
When they travel to the past , there are more difficulties faced by them.

Let's read this book and enjoy the captivating story of this book.

Acknowledgements

I acknowledge this book to my parents and all the people who supports me to write this book .

Not dedicate to my parents , I am dediacte this book into my dedication to write this book . Fine , listen my short story , one day in night , I suddenly awake up and decide to publish a book . my age is like 10 years so , if any mmistake is done in this book or any grammatical error in this book , so please forget me . Thanks for your support.

Prologue

Consider one thing that you go to adventure of time travel to save humanity so , how you clarify.. Are you nervous on the point of that incident ....read this book to know about the situatation of Lily and Jim.

1

HOOK WARNING

A warning from Professor Hooks to Jim and Lily about time travel !

" Oh what is this? " Professor Hook said .

"I never expect this from the next generation …I will discuss this from Jim and Lily."

With a red light and the echoing sound of an alarm …Professor Hooks will be very disappointed . This alarm is not a simple alarm , this alarm will ring when a disaster comes . What is this disaster ? Let's know about it !

" I think that I will talk to Jim about this incident , and later Jim will discuss it with Lily," Hook imagined .

Professor will call Jim immediately and call him in the lab .

"Hey , Jim What's Up ! "

" I am fine , professor ; what's about you ? "

"I want to discuss a major incident with you ; come into the lab immediately , Jim . "

"Sure , Professor ! "

Within 10 minutes , Jim comes to the Hook's Lab. Jim is looking so happy and he wears a red shirt and blue jeans ; looking like a handsome guy.

Now , this happiness will soon turn into sorrow . Jim joyfully enters the lab and goes to meet the professor.

"Hey, professor , what are the major concerns ? "

"That's so big "

"What professor ?"

"Look at the screen , this is the world of 2079, those countries which is marked as a red and orange are fully addicted and controlled by a harmful device and an powerful device "

"How these countries peoples will addicted and how is this possible "

" I collected some information about this . "

" Please tell me "

" This device named as the 76B and this is controlled by the main powerhouse called 6790A , it is a powerhouse that are controlled by one organisation so,

When this powerhouse activates , it makes a powerful magnetic wave and this magnetic wave will activate the 76B , 77B , 78B and 79B .

When these are activated , it makes an addictive radiation that addicted all peoples in the world . "

" Where this setup located "

" Santa Clara , California ! "

" How can I helps you , professor ..in this case "

" Come in 2 days , I will invent the time travel machine , and then you will go to the future "

" Any instructions , professor ! "

" I will tell you after 2 days. "

" Sure , professor ! "

3

2

CONVINCING LILY

After discussion with the professor , Jim thinks that he can't travel in the future on his own . He must talk to her best friend for this scenario.With the hope , he will go to the lily house .

"Oh ! I forgot that around 5 :00 PM , she will go to the park today " . Jim thinks .

Jim suddenly remembers that and takes a taxi and goes to Silicon BC Park. after reaching there ; he started searching the lily everywhere.

"Hey , Lily .. how are you ? "

"Oh ! Jim , I am fine and you are as rare as once in a blue moon " !

" Oh really my cutie pie ".

"Yes ! "

" I want to discuss a important thing to you "

"Yes , sure "

" At 4:00 AM , suddenly my phone rings and the professor Hooks call me suddenly in his lab ; then , I were going in the Hook's Lab ..then Professor told me this scenario ;

Professor Hook's said , "Look at the screen , this is the world of 2079, those countries which is marked as a red and orange are fully addicted and controlled by a harmful device and an powerful device "

Lily said , " But how ? "

Jim said ,"You just need to know this, Lily - we'll have to go through a very difficult path now. Professor Hooks will tell us everything tomorrow. Will you leave me in this difficult time? I swear on humanity and my own promise, you have to come with me.

"Think about it, Lily - what will happen to those people who are completely addicted? Just imagine... think about it."

The convincing style of the Jim is unique and like a preplanned idea. I think that this unique style must make Lily feel so emotional . Let's take a look at the expression and response of the Cutie girl .

" As you wish , Jim ; I am ready to go with you at this dangerous moment ".

" Oh thanks ; Lily ...we will meet the professor hooks tomorrow at 4:00 PM .

" Ok ! Jim "

3

TIME TRAVEL IN FUTURE

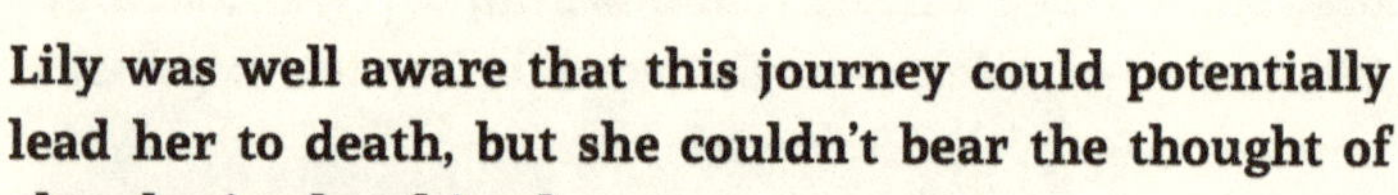

Lily was well aware that this journey could potentially lead her to death, but she couldn't bear the thought of abandoning her friend.

With a smiling face and a heart filled with fear, she convinced herself for the journey.

"Hey ; Lily ! The time has arrived to meet professor Hooks ; Shall we depart now ? "

" Sure ! Jim "

They depart at 4: 30 PM and then take a taxi to Brooklyn Bridge .
The Hook's Lab near the Brooklyn Bridge.

After 15 Minutes ; they reach the Hook's Lab ! . Professor Hooks work on a
massive, translucent orb, partially blue and red in hue, was encased within a green
circle.

A brilliant radiation light gleamed on top of it. The orb

had a glass-like surface,

allowing visibility from both sides, and was adorned with numerous buttons.

Inside, there were two seats. The man stood in front of the hue ; it looked like a

tiny speck.

"What is this ? ; this looks like a time machine ?"

" Yes, Lily ! Let's go to ask Professor Hooks."

Lily and Jim go near the professor and ask what they will do now ?

Lily is entirely unaware that she will be going to time travel now .They will go near the professor and ask about the next move of the chess game !

"Hey ; professor, what is the next move?"

" Look at this huge hue ; this is a time

machine and you have only 72 hours to save humanity and diffuse the 76B !

After 72 hours ; you will automatically come to this world. "

"Professor, could you please clarify our destination and the logistics of our arrival? What challenges can we expect to encounter?

Additionally, could you reveal the identity of the organization responsible for these events?

Should we also prepare ourselves with defensive measures, such as weapons?" Jim said .

"I've tried very hard, Jim ; but I couldn't find out anything about that organization or anything else. Look, Jim, this is a chess game where you're moving a pawn, but the knight appears from the next army. You must have listened to my instructions carefully because in this chess game, there's only the king and queen, not the entire army."

"Sure ; professor . Now you can give the instructions . "

"Listen this carefully ; Jim and Lily "

" • You have only 72 hours to defeat that organisation .

You must avoid the paradoxes of the time but I think that paradox must happen when you enter the future .

As possible ; you will not kill anyone because it creates a paradox.

When you enters the time machine ; you enters without any metal object because the frame attached the metal object very forcefully "

" I give you this locket ; when you need me ; you will press this icon ; I appear digitally through AR " .

Professor gives the instructions to Jim and says that this time is best for time travel .

Professor opens the door of the time machine and Lily and Jim enter the time machine .

The Green circle that covered the machine is rotating and Boom ! Jim and Lily will disappear.

One thing that the professor forgot to tell him is the name of the head of this organisation and how this machine will diffuse .

There's no other source of communication between them , now wait for Jim's Call !

4
THE UNKNOWN WORLD OF FUTURE

.. Scenario like this ..

Everything was normal ; but after they appeared , the extremely hot light glowed and spread on the highway.

After they reach the future ; the only motive is to find that organisation that operates 76B.

After 10 minutes of their arrival ; the time machine will vanish. Lily and Jim have only 70 hours to defeat and shut down the 76B because after this ; they are unable to control the spread of waves by 76B.

After 10 minutes ; they will go to a resident place and stay at night .

" Jim ; we have only 70 hours "

" Yes ; Lily "

" But how do we find that organisation because we have no clue and processor. "

" If any organisation does this so simply ; they don't allow you to enter that organisation ; we will find all organisations who do not allow everyone to enter".

"Yes Jim ; and that organisation is tech- related that's the reason they will run the software of 76B " !

" Where is the most tech related work occured in the USA ? "

"I don't know , Jim "

" Search on the Internet ! "

" Listen ; Jim , according to the internet and recent data ; the most industries that have tech or IT related work will reside in Silicon Valley , Santa Clara , Los San Jose . "

"We are exactly where we need to be."

" Search all the It Industries who will best known for the tech work in santa clara "

" According to internet , Jim "

IT Industries in Santa Working Hours
Santa Clara IT Opened (8 to 10)
Robotic VICTIM IT Not Reported 404
San Jose IT Not reported 404
"These are the Top 3 IT industries in Santa Clara in which two are not reported on the internet.

The last reported in 2074 by head Mark ".

"We need to Investigate 3 industries and ya ; be ensure that we have weapons to fight " .

5
INVESTIGATION

Lily and Jim knew very well that one of the two companies was operating the device. They had to find out who it was as soon as possible.

Because of less time ; they play their next move of chess. This move is unknown for the pawn to become queen in the next move.

They decide to visit and figure out the IT company named " Robotic Victim IT " in Santa Clara.

"Hey ; Jim , I think that we will investigate the "Robotic Victim IT " firstly because it is near our residence".

" Sure ! Lily ; ".

" Prepare weapons for emergency ".

" Yes ! I already prepared for it . "

Lily and Jim prepared the weapons and took a taxi to 68 Mile Road , Silicon Valley , Santa Clara where the Robotic victim IT industry was located.

After 20 minutes of travelling ; Lily and Jim will reach their destination .

" Lily ! Look at this ; what is this ? "

" Yes Jim ! "

Actually, Lily and Jim will see the company and they will be astonished. This looks like that this is firstly designed by any modus operandi .

The company is surrounded by machines and the flying carpets like airplanes. The mouse darts for cleaning and the robots which are actually used for fighting as well as work on technology.

Lily and Jim will be totally confused and it looks like this company is ad hoc for fighting .

After this , they will know by internet that this company is operated by a person named ' Mark Clinton ' . They went inside the company and met with ' Mark Clinton '.

" Who are you ; man ? " Mark asked them.

" Hey ; my name is Jim Clinton and my friend's name is Lily Brown ".

" How can I assist you , Mr. Clinton ."

" Actually , we are searching for a technical issue and we want to take a check of your company ".

Mark looked at them with intense anger, but perhaps Lily's charm worked on him. He thought for a while, then somehow he agreed in agreement.

Lily and Jim will free for the next move.

" We don't have enough time to investigate each company . "

" So , "

" I will investigate one side of the company and you investigate the other side, so it 's easy to investigate the whole company in less time ."

"Yes ! Jim ; this is a better idea ."

Jim and Lily will investigate the whole company but any machine or any work didn't indicate the work 76B.

Jim and Lily verify all the machines with the image of 76B that is provided by Mr. Hooks. Any machinery does not indicate this !

" I think that this company does not operate the 76B " . Jim said to Lily.

" Yes, we will go to investigate the next company ".

After that, Jim and Lily said their goodbyes to Mark and set off towards their next path in their modus operandi.

" Jim , I have a doubt in the investigation " .

" But why ? "

"I don't know why, but when I was going to investigate , I heard a lot of commotion coming from within the grounds.

It felt like there was something inside the ground that was being hidden from me.

And when I approached an employee during my investigation, I asked him about it.

For some reason, he became a bit nervous and started stuttering. It seemed like what he was saying wasn't entirely true.

Anyway, I went to another employee, and he flat out denied that there was nothing inside the ground in our company.

But what was weird was everyone's reaction when I asked about it. I think there's something fishy going on, Jim. There was something there that maybe we overlooked. Lily said to Jim .

By the way ; they continued talking and they eventually reached their next destination ,' San Jose IT '.

According to the Internet ; this company is operated by ' Jack Nova ' who is a bright entrepreneur from Los San Jose .

"Hey, Mr. Jack Nova , Myself Jim Clinton and here's my friend Lily Brown. "

" How Can I assist you ? "

" Actually , we are searching for a technical issue and we want to take a check of your company ".

"Yes, Sure ! ".

Lily and Jim will meet Jack and repeat the same line that they spoke in Mark's Company.

Jack gives permission to investigate their company . Jack was a person with a kind heart and a passionate nature.

Then, they will investigate the company in the same way that they did in Mark's Company. But there's nothing in that company about the harmful device.

Jack observed them very closely and realized that no genuine technician would be tinkering with the machines in such a manner. Jack understood very well that these people were not technicians. There was something else going on.

" Maybe these people are searching for the 76B in my company " .

Jack will say loudly ,"Hey man , please come ! ".

Lily and Jim will come near Jack. Jack says," Are you searching for the 76B device ".

As soon as they heard this , they pointed their guns to Jack's head.

Now Jack was certain that they were finding 76B. With a trembling voice, Jack said,

"Listen to me, I'm also against 76B. That's a reason you won't find anything in my company that's against 76B.

And yes, I also know which organization controls 76B. You people are far behind in gathering information, but I know everything about it.

It seems you don't understand that we only have 19 hours and 45 minutes left. So, don't waste time and put

down your guns. Then I'll tell you everything I know."

" Okay ! "

" Listen to me , 76B is such an addictive device that is controlled by a company named Mark Victim IT.

" What ? Is it true , Jim exclaimed. "

"Yes , and the head of this company is Mark Clinton . "

"But we had gone to the same company for investigation before deciding to investigate here, yet we didn't find anything suspicious."

" Will you investigate in the underground Lab. "

"What ! That company also has an underground lab, but as far as we knew, when Lily asked an employee about the underground lab, the employee directly refused it and said that there's no underground lab in their company."

"No, the company saved itself."

"The underground lab has 76B which is operated by 6790A and not for 76B. After 19 hours , the 6790A is activated and its magnetic field activates the device 76B, 77B , 78B , 79B and these devices later control the humans !.

"What can we do now ?"

"We must fight , for our rights , for our freedom!"

"Yes !"

"Look at this map ; this map has 76B location ; this device will be shut down by a secret 5 Digit code and we must fight with Mark for this code."

"Can we take the help of the police force ?"

"We need to prove and give the exact location of 76B !"

"So, Make a plan to defeat the mark and its intentions ."

"But I have a query for you ?"

Yes ! " Jack replied

" Why does Mark want to control all the humans? What is the reason behind this ?" Jim said

"A long time ago, something sad happened to Mark. His parents, Lily Brown and Jim Clinton, were trying to help people and go on a dangerous mission to save humanity. But Lily died on that mission. She was shot in the heart.

Mark was very sad. His father, Jim, was also very sad. He loved Lily so much that he died a month later. Mark was left all alone.

Since then, Mark has been trying to find the people who hurt his mom. He wants justice for her death. He's still very sad and angry about what happened. Since he promised to destroy humanity." Jack explained

"My name is Jim Clinton and my friend is Lily brown ... .Ha..ha..ha ! " Jim said

"It is a coincidence , Jim but we focus on defeating Mark as soon as possible". Jack said

"After an hour , prepare yourself and we meet in Clara 5.0 Park." Jack said.

6
FIRST PHASE OF WAR

❦

With only 16 hours left, Jim and Lily get ready for their next move. Jim was very nervous, but he was trying to reassure Lily that they would win this fight no matter what.

On the other side , Jack will also get ready to take the king by its pawn. Jack will know that maybe those people will help me to defeat Mark. Jack will go to his weapon room and practice each shot and gun with the next power.

"Yahoo! What a shot ! "

Smashed...crack..crack..crack !

"What a shot , Jack ! "

Jack will be fully prepared and going to take some rest .

On the other hand , Jim will know that their old technology weapons cannot defeat the new technology weapons.

Because of that , he will take the locket which is given by Professor Hooks and press the red button inside it.

Ssshhh , the AR view of Professor Hooks comes out from the locket.

"What happened , Mr."

"Professor, I have a problem !"

" What ? " Said politely.

"Professor, As we know that our old techno weapons can't defeat the newest techno weapons, ya , the newest weapons have ice power and fire power and so on.

What will we do now ?"

"I know ; Jim and I have a solution to this.

Go near Clara 3.0 park and there's a tunnel that is covered with a reddish brown cloth and that tunnel is near the Banyan tree.

Go under the tunnel and verify yourself with pass 1467 and verify your face then , practice and choose all the best weapons in those categories ".

"Thanks a lot , professor ! "

After that , Lily and Jim will make a plan to go near Clara 3.0 park . He takes a taxi to Clara 3.0 and reaches its destination after 15 minutes.

"This is the exact place where the Professor gave us the address of the tunnel."

"Look at that ! There's a banyan tree. "

They ran towards the banyan tree and reached near it .

There's a reddish brown cloth covering a circle.

They unwrap the cloth and find the circle that has a fingerprint scanner and a password locker.

They enter the password that is given by the professor and they need to verify.

After fingerprint and face verification ; they go under the tunnel.

When they entered the tunnel, they were greeted by a robot with dazzling lights.

The robot was extremely helpful. The tunnel was enormous, stretching far and wide, and was equipped

with a vast array of guns with the best technology. Lily and Jim felt confident that they could now defeat Mark.

They began testing each gun, and after testing, they even tried using every piece. Lily and Jim's confidence grew as they witnessed the robot's efficiency.

As per promise , Lily and Jim take a taxi from Clara 3.0 to Clara 5.0. After 10 minutes of travelling, they reached Clara 3.0 park.

Jack will also be there. Lily and Jim go near Jack and discuss the next move .

"Hey ! Jack , what's next ! "

"Understand this very clearly: what you think is happening is not as simple as it seems. Defeating Mark is no ordinary task; it can cost us our lives. He's incredibly powerful, to the point where even the entire police force and military combined can't hurt him.

But still, we will fight, and listen carefully, I have a plan. We will work according to this plan."

"What's the plan according to you ! "

"Listen carefully , we will fight Mark in a separate way.

Firstly Lily will go to the entrance door and fight the securities and other people and on the other side , Jim..you will fight with Mark , but remember one thing , you can't take him down alone, so your only option is to distract him and engage in a fight where you won't get hurt too much.

On the other hand , I will try to shut down the 76B , 77B and so on ! But I think I only try to shut down 76B, not other devices.

Remember, things are not always as they seem ! " Jack said !

"Ok ! Jack , I will fight and I promise to you that we will win this chess game ."

As per plan , they need to work separately and go in a particular way.

Lily takes a taxi to Mark Victim IT and goes to the entrance of that company.

Actually, Lily was supposed to carry out her task according to the plan, but for some reason, she was feeling a bit nervous.

However, something happened that motivated her so much that she felt she could not only take down this company but also anyone who dared to harm humanity.

Lily thought she would fight for her planet and humanity, just like her father had fought in a war and sacrificed his life.

By successfully completing this mission, she would destroy the entire company, and her father would be proud of her.

Suddenly Lily remembered the promise that she made with her father.

Lily's Father said at the time of death ,"Lily, even if you have to sacrifice your own life, you must do it, because saving this world is your first duty."

Lily remembered this and with a drop of tears , she continued her journey.

With a new fate , Lily will reach the Mark Victim IT and look at many people and guards to secure the main entrance of the company.

Lily with new motivation go near the one guard and said ,

" Hey, guard ! " with a dangerous voice

"Yes; miss...ahhhh".

She shot the guard and within the second attack of any guard ; she took the two flame guns and a freeze grenade and with two flame guns , they shot the people and guard.

She took the grenade and threw it at the main entrance and with total attack , 67 people died on the spot.

"Thsh..Tshs............booom ! Save us Save us ! " Sounds echoing in the main door.

Like everywhere it is full of smoke and dust , a person who is standing there does not have a he ran and put the safety alarm .

The safety alarm sounds 'Beep Beep' echoing everywhere.

Because of this echoing sound , Lily has faced more soldiers but she fights encouragely towards them.

On the other hand , Jim's task was to fight with Mark because of echoing sound everywhere ; every soldier ran towards the main door and Jim was free to defeat mark.

The beeping sound made Jim realize that he wouldn't get a better opportunity to confront Mark.

So, without wasting time, he started finding Mark, who, after hearing the emergency safety alarm, was moving towards 76B with a furious expression.

Mark's face was worth seeing. On one hand, he was showing anger, for finding who had done all this... and on the other hand, he was worried and slightly scared because this was a sudden uprising, and Mark had no idea about it.

Mark had taken a dangerous-looking weapon in his hand, which Jim was unaware of. The weapon was glowing with a greenish-blue light and blue radiation.

Jim has a flame weapon and a green grenade that helps him to fight with Mark.

Jim thought and fired the flame gun and green grenade towards Mark. Mark will be unknown for this sudden attack. Mark was hurt in this attack.

Mark looked at Jim with bloodshot eyes that seemed to be redder than blood... and then thought for a moment, and a loud voice echoed.

The voice was like someone had thrown 3-4 grenades there. Jim fell back and got stunned.

As soon as Jim fell, he made his best comeback, delivering a dialogue like a film hero, and with a comeback, he shot Mark's hand with both guns. Mark was knocked out for 2 minutes with 7 flames.

Jim realized that it was time to help Jack. So, he ran and started searching for 76B everywhere.

"Garr garr " the sound comes from under the ground.

Jack had told him that there was an underground tunnel, and the sound of machines was coming from below. Therefore, he quickly followed the sound and reached the underground location of 76B.

As soon as Jim arrived, Jack looked at him and said,

'What happened? Did something go wrong? Why did you come here?'

Jim replied, 'Nothing, I shot Mark and he's unconscious, but he can come here anytime... so you need to do what you need to do quickly.'

'Okay,' Jack replied, looking very worried. In his anxiety at peak, he prepared to diffuse 76B.

76B is a huge device that is covered with a green radiation power band and the security is at peak. In the top of 76B , a blue smoke continuously comes out from it.

The 76B is made up of hard galvanised metal that is covered as a blue and Jack tried to diffuse this.

Suddenly, Jack saw that In 76B , there's an entrance but it is locked by any type of password.

Jim tries to open the password.

"Oh! shit ..what is the password for this ! Maybe it is the name of the company."

Jim enters the password with hope but the password is incorrect.

Boom! Tshs ! A beam of radiation hit Jack's Arm.

Jack understood that if he enters the wrong password, a beam of gin hits me .

Jack has only 1 attempt because the machine is set to be only 2 attempts.

Jack thinks and realises that the password may have the name of Mark's mom.

So, with risk life and limb , the jack enters the password .

"*****Correct password ! authentication completed!"

"Oh , so the password is 'Lily Brown'.

"Ahhh..." Mark attacks Jack suddenly.

As soon as Jim saw Mark who was attacking Jack, he immediately countered with a powerful blow, knocking Mark down.

Jack, seizing the opportunity, engulfed Mark in flames, which surrounded him for a while.

Lily, Jim and Jack know the password of the devices and Mark was unknown about that but unfortunately, Jim and Jack cannot diffuse the device

7
SECOND PHASE OF WAR

Jim and Jack know the password to diffuse that device but unfortunately, they
can't diffuse that device because of the sudden attack of Mark.

**Actually, Jack didn't have the upper pawn to back suddenly but he was playing a
clever card .
He wanted to catch Mark off guard, when he least expected a fight, and wasn't
prepared for an all-out war.**

**After all, 'a stitch in time saves nine,' and Jack knew that if they didn't strike
now, Mark would become an unstoppable force.**

**'Give him an inch, and he'll take a mile,' Jack thought to himself.
So, Jack's plan was to have Lily blow the whistle on Mark**

by informing the police
and military about his terror activity. Meanwhile, Jack
and Jim would burn the midnight oil, taking advice from
the professor and fine-tuning their preparations.
This midnight oil later burned the mark completely with
the redemption.
They would test their new guns, making sure they were
locked and loaded for the
final showdown. Ha Ha ...Ha .

When Lily sounded the alarm and informed police , the
police would join the war,
launching a second attack on Mark.
This would be a classic case of 'divide and conquer,' where
Mark would be caught
between two fires, unable to cope with the pressure.

'When the going gets tough, the tough get going,' Jack
thought, and he was
confident that their combined forces would be too much
to handle for Mark.
Then, and only then, would they go for the final war. It
would be a 'do-or-die'
battle, where only the strongest would survive.
But Jack was confident that with their careful planning
and preparation, they
would emerge victorious in the end.

According to Jack's plan , Lily takes a taxi and goes to the
military and police
office and is informed about Mark's conspiracy.

"Hey, officer ! I just wanna say something."

"Why not, mam ! "

Then, Lily tells everything about Mark and Mark's plan to kill humanity.

"But how do I believe your argument !"

" Here's a proof of my argument".

"Lily shows a pic that she clicked when Mark attacked Jack."

"Oh ! What a dangerous thing this is ! "

"Yes, professor ; we need to save humanity as soon as possible."

In 2 minutes, police informed military officers in Los San Jose and went to Mark's
Victim IT.

"BUT, I THINK THAT THIS FORCE ARE NOT SUFFICIENT TO DEFEAT MARK. SO,
WE NEED THE HELP OF NEIGHBOUR CITY !". Officer said.

Officers requested another city 'Evergreen' to take part in this war.
'Evergreen government accepted this request and not Evergreen's force, however
'Evergreen' provided weapons to Los San Jose from 'Silver Creek'.

The police and military had perhaps taken such a move

that Mark would later feel
like a pawn had captured the queen.

They had finally managed to 'get the upper hand' and were now in a position to
dictate the terms of the game.
    The police and military were now likely to be enough to end Mark's game, and this
war was likely ....boom.

It seemed like they were 'pulling out all the stops' to ensure Mark's downfall.
Seeing such a large police force, will Mark get scared? Or will this police force
also fail to defeat Mark?

After the decision of the police forces , an announcement was made in the airport
by the government.

The announcement was that , "Any citizen found attempting to exit the country
through any airport or utilizing any mode of transportation shall be liable to a
punishment of imprisonment for a term of twenty (20) years, in addition to any other
penalties as may be deemed applicable."

Also, the same announcement is given by other neighbourhood cities that help Los
San Jose like Evergreen city and Silver Greek country.
"NOTICE IS HEREBY GIVEN that any person, being
be prescribed by law." These are the same lines that are

announced by the
countries.

Only 5 hours were left now, and whatever had to be done,
had to be done within
those 5 hours, because if 76, 77, 78, 79 (B) were activated,
then the entire
world's military and police would not be able to defeat
Mark.
As the saying goes, 'time and tide wait for none,' and Mark
knew he had to act
fast. As soon as the government made the announcement,
Mark understood very
well that the police had found out about his plans.

And he also knew very well that all this was the doing of
those three. But Mark
didn't have enough time to find them and punish them,
because the police would
arrive any moment.

After all, 'when the cat's away, the mice will play,' and
Mark knew t...
This was just like in chess, when after checkmate , the
queen and bishop
surrounded the king from the sides to checkmate.
The police and military had closed in on Mark's company
like a vice, leaving no
room for escape.

Mark's men were vastly outnumbered, and it seemed like
only a matter of time
before they were overpowered. The sound of sirens filled

the air, and the flashing
lights of the police cars illuminated the darkening sky.
Mark's world was closing in around him, and he knew he had to think fast if he
wanted to survive.

The police and military forces had completely taken over Mark Victim IT. An
announcement was made by the military and police officers,
"The Police Force has discovered your illegal activities and has surrounded you from all...
But Mark was not willing to give up on his dreams so, he took out a flame gun and
a powerful GR5 and launched a counterattack on the police and military officers.
The flame gun injured 20 police officers and killed 7, while the GR5 destroyed 6
tanks, 8 aircraft, and killed 10 military officers.

The police and military started continuous firing.
600 tanks, 990 aircraft, and 1500 police officers opened fire. The entire city was
filled with chaos due to the firing.
Mark, realizing the situation, decided to use his remaining resources and activate
a shield.

However, as the old saying goes, "Pride comes before a fall,".

Mark's shield may not be able to withstand the intense firing for as long as he thought.

The sky was filled with smoke and dust.

She met with Jim and Jack and briefed them on the situation, knowing that they
had to come up with a new plan to counter Mark's shield and bring an end to the
chaos.

The police and military force will continuously attack at the shield . The shield was
destroyed by the attack of the police firing .

When the shield was destroyed , it made a huge sound like above 180 Decibels
that make deaf some police officers who stand near that field deaf .

But with that disability , they fight in the war continuously and attack the shield.
Because of the destroyed shield , the police officers and military officers are
allowed to enter the company.
    The tank or aircraft cannot enter the company.
Like the quit india movement and the revolt of 1857 , the huge masses of people.

"What can we do ? " A police officer says the military.

"Firstly, we wait for a while and I have a anti- poisonous mark so, wear it and we attack
the company and arrest them. "

"Sir, Can we kill or arrest them ?"

"Look, this situation depends on whether he is powerful or weak. But as far as I can
tell, he seems to be extremely powerful. So, I'm giving you the order to 'Sight and
Shoot', fire at will as soon as you see him."

"OKAY!"

Everyone wears the anti- poisonous mask and goes to the company's entrance.
After they enter the company , a mass of people ie. 60 to 90 people, attack the
police officers and with the 'SIGHT AND SHOOT ' order, every officer fires and
fires at the people .

With a great struggle , the police defeat this mass of people
.

The actual war had started now. The police had defeated 60 to 90 people, but
another big threat was coming. Many more people came to fight the police with
many weapons.

The police were strong too, and they won the fight. After a while , everything
seemed to be quiet .

It seemed like nothing had happened. The police went to

find 76B, thinking only a
few people were left.
    But something felt wrong, the quietness of that place was
like the calm before a big storm.

Suddenly, a huge fireball fell on the police. It was as big as a house and had
black as it coverning in an outer part ; red as it is a flame that surrounded a
firewall , and green as it is an inner flame part of the fireball.

The fireball is so massive and the speed of the fireball is so high. After the fireball attack on the police officers ; we know that many police officers were killed and burned.

In this game of chess, the white team is left with only the king, queen, bishop,
and 10 pawns, while the black team has its entire army to attack.

However, there's a twist - the pawns in the black team's army are slightly weaker
than the white team's pawns.

And the white team King and queen is slightly weaker than the black's team king.
Now, the white chess pawns are probably gone, and the 10 police officers who
were guarding the company exterior realized that they couldn't defeat the enemy
alone and would need any support.

As the saying goes, 'one grain of rice cannot break a stone.'

8
FINAL PHASE OF WAR

They knew that if they didn't act fast, Mark would become so powerful that the whole world government couldn't defeat him.

As the saying goes, "time waits for no one," and they had to make the most of the little time they had left.

They decided to go to Clara 3.0 park to come up with a new plan. But when they arrived, they found out that the park was not just a normal park.

It was a secret weapon store, hidden behind a layer of trees and plants.

The team was surprised and excited by this discovery and again in chess, a pawn can once again become a queen and able to checkmate the king.

They knew that with these advanced weapons, they might have a chance to defeat Mark. But they also knew that they had to be careful. As the saying goes, "pride comes before a fall," and they didn't want to underestimate Mark's power.

In chess, when a player is in a difficult position, they often try to sacrifice some of their pieces to gain an advantage.

The police and military team was in a similar situation. They had to think carefully about their next move and be willing to make some sacrifices in order to win.

So, In the Clara 3.0 park , the police officers go to the underground weapon store and practise the shooting .

"Splash ; crack ; boom ! these sound comes from the underground weapon store. "

"Yahoo! Nice shot ! "

On the other side , Jim , Jack and Lily prepare on Clara 3.0 park. The police officers prepare in Clara Weapon 2 and Jim and Lily prepare in Clara Weapon 1.

Jim said ,"Now, we don't have much time left; we can say that we only have 1 hour left.

We should head out to war now because we've been practicing for the last 5 hours. Now, it's time for us to go out there and defeat Mark."

"You're right Jim ! " Jack replied.

Jim and Jack going out from the Clara Weapon 1.

On the other hand ; the police officers also make a plan and select the special guns and come out from the Clara Weapon 2 .

Coincidentally, the police officers and Jim, Jack, and Lily met up. Jim was shocked and surprised, wondering how the police and military were here because he thought they were still at Mark Victim IT... but he had no idea that out of the entire force, only these 10 people had survived.

"Hey, police officers ! how are you here ?"

"Means !"

" I think that you will go to fight with Mark !"

"Hmm......!" **Then , a police commissioner got emotional and tears came out of his eyes.**

Then, the police officer told all the things that they faced !

Jim said ," It looks like that it is Mark's modus operandi but after the fiasco , we can't give up.

Police officers said with tears ,"We were at least 1200 people, but when we went to Mark's Victim IT, a lot happened.

As soon as the police officers were about to enter the company, Mark put up a shield. When the shield diffused, there was a massive sound that left the people standing nearby deaf, and some even died.

Then, as the police officers moved forward, they encountered poisonous gas. When they went to attack, a huge crowd of people attacked them. Then, out of nowhere, a massive fireball attacked, killing many police officers.

The fireball was large and its impact was not countable. The police officers who survived were left shaken and wounded. Now, you're our only hope. The tanks are still standing there, continuously fighting.

We don't have much time left, so let's hurry. As the old saying , "Time is of the essence," and every minute counts. We can't afford to waste any more time.

We also know that Mark's powers are growing stronger by the minute, and if we don't act fast, he'll become unstoppable. As the saying goes, "strike while the iron is hot," and we need to take advantage of this opportunity before it's too late.

Let's move quickly and come up with a plan to defeat Mark once and for all."

This hurts them a lot. They are prepared and take a taxi ; and go to the Mark's Victim IT .

After 2 minutes , they reached their destination.

Jim knows that something is strange about Mark's guard.

So, he again uses the locket that is given by Hooks and when Jim presses the button in the middle of it , a greenish- blue light comes out and the AR view of the professor comes out .

"What happened , Jim ? " Professor said

" Professor, when we shoot at the guards that are from the opposite side, they die after we shoot 5-6 flames, but if the guard is a human, only one flame is enough to kill them. "Jim presents their query.

"Rightly thought, Jim, but don't say that you're in the future, rather in the present.

The technology there will be far more advanced than ours in 2024.

So, it's possible that they're not humans, but human-like robots. And as far as I know, every robot's main operating system is located on its belly. So, this time, try to attack the belly side."

"Thanks for guiding me ! ".

Jim shuts down the locket and the AR (Augmented Reality) vanishes.

Jim had now fully understood that this was the final battle, and they would defeat Mark together.

Without wasting any time, they headed towards Mark Victim IT.

As they arrived, they saw that some of their officers were still fighting. They had only one hour to do what they had to do.

There wasn't even enough time to make a plan, so this battle wasn't pre-planned at all. Jim shouted, 'Attack them in such a way that no one is left!' Jack understood that Jim was extremely angry.

"The police officers who were fighting there, Jack took out the weapons to help them. Jack took out a weapon that was extremely deadly.

The mouth of the weapon looked like a falcon, and the back was very sharp. Its shape looked very deadly, with a sky blue color and a dark blue outer coating.

Jack, who was in anger, took out the falcon gun and shot the guards in the belly ... As soon as Jack shot, a blue radiation came out of the falcon gun, and that radiation killed 10 people in one attack in one go.

But when the guards died, no blood came out, instead, sparks started flying; this proved Professor Hooks' suspicion correct... These people were not humans, but robots.

Because of this, Jack released 4 radiations at once and knocked down 56 guards... and attacked their belly, which saved the police officers, and Jack created chaos in the company again.

When Jack was showing such bravery, Jim couldn't stay behind. So, Jim took out his Eagle gun, and Lily took out her Ice and Fire gun. 10 police officers also took out their guns.

Jack had already attacked with his Falcon gun, but now Jack, Lily, and Jim were searching for Mark.

As soon as the entire team entered the company, the security guards, who were robots, attacked them like magnets attract iron.

The police officers took out their guns, and 14 of them started non-stop firing at the robots' bellies. There were more than 100 robots.

Jim and Jack stopped there, and Lily went to search for Mark. Lily went to find Mark.

Jim and Jack took out their Falcon gun and Eagle gun to help the police officers.

As you know, the Falcon gun emits blue gamma radiation. The Eagle gun is similar but emits a rainbow beam with VIBGYOR colors and is 10 times more powerful than the Falcon gun.

Its design is similar to the Falcon gun, with an eagle-like mouth, black interior, and VIBGYOR-colored veins. Its back end is also very sharp.

Regarding its damage, the Eagle gun's beam divides into 7 rays. One beam can burn 100 people into ashes in just one move, in a nanosecond.

Due to its extreme danger, whoever uses it must be careful, or they might also get affected.

Since there were around 100 guards, Jim asked everyone to stop shooting. He said, 'Give me silence; one beam is enough for these people.'

Then, he fired two beams, and the people running in front turned into ashes in 0.002 nanoseconds.

Jim's confidence was skyrocketing, and he thought that now Mark wouldn't be able to escape alive.

After all this, Jim, Jack, and the 14 police officers moved forward. Lily was still searching for Mark. They made a plan that Lily and Jack would distract Mark, while the police officers would fight off any guards. Jim would go to diffuse devices 76, 77, 78, and 79B.

As Jack and Lily went to find Mark, Jim went to locate the devices. Suddenly, Mark appeared with his weapons, ready to attack. A police officer warned them about Mark's attack. As Mark attacked, the 14 police officers started firing at him. But Mark took out a strange-looking gun and shot the police officers, turning them into ashes in one second.

Mark then attacked Jack with gamma radiation. Jack took out his Falcon gun to defend himself, but Mark's radiation was too powerful, and the Falcon gun broke into four pieces. Lily then froze Mark using her Ice gun, but it wouldn't last long.

Jack and Lily quickly ran to Jim, who was diffusing the devices. Jack took the Eagle gun from Jim, hoping it would be stronger than Mark's gun. Just then, Mark appeared and turned Jim into a ball of fire as he was diffusing device 76B.

Mark then fired gamma radiation at Jack, who defended himself using the Eagle gun's VIBGYOR radiation. The two radiations clashed, causing a massive explosion. Mark's gun was destroyed, and he was shocked.

In a fit of rage, Mark attacked Jim with another Falcon gun. Jim had no shield or defense, and the gun's speed was too fast. But Lily, who loved Jim more than her own life, sacrificed herself to save Jim. She took the full force of the gamma radiation, and her body turned into a volcano, eventually killing her.

Jim was devastated, and his heart was broken. But then, a strange thing happened - Mark disappeared. Jack was shocked, and Jim was unable to process what had happened.

Just then, Jack realized that the devices were about to activate. Jim quickly diffused devices 76B, 77, 78, and 79B within seconds. Jack was relieved, but he was also sad that Lily had sacrificed her life to save humanity.

Mark's disappearance remained a mystery, and Jack couldn't understand what had happened. Jim returned home, still grieving for Lily, and went back to 2025.

The Mystery Of Mark

Jim was strong, but Lily was his first love. As they say, "First love is blind and never forgetting." After Lily left on her mission, Jim began to cry uncontrollably.

His heart was shattered into a hundred pieces. Jim wasn't capable of handling the situation, so Jack had to intervene. Jim sat alone, tears streaming down his face, reminiscing about Lily and the memories they shared.

He remembered how Lily took care of him when he had a fever in December. Jack comforted him, and it was time for Jim to move on. Taking a deep breath, Jim stepped into the present, carrying the weight of his sorrow.

This story captures the pain of lost love and the struggle to move on. Jim's heart still beats for Lily, and the memories of their time together linger. With Jack's support, Jim finds the strength to face the present, but his heart remains tied to the past.

Author Note :And one final twist to end this entire book: Mark's parents were none other than Lily Brown and Jim Clinton, and everything that happened was a revenge for Lily's death. That's why Mark destroyed humanity. And remember, time travel has occurred. If I were to tell you everything, what would you do? So, think about why this happened. And yes, the answer is ithis book... don't think it's somewhere else. So, this was the story of Lily and Jim, in which humanity came to an end, but with a pain that will linger.

- K.Suryansh Tripathi

This novel "Time Dilemma " that subnamed is "The Time Travel Paradox " is written by Author "Suryansh Tripathi".

Suryansh Tripathi was born on 23 January 2011 and loved writing in their childhood. He wrote his first story " A bride with red saree" at the age of 7 when he studied in class 7th.

Presently , Suryansh Tripathi lived in Kanpur Nagar at the age of 14 years.

He studied in class 9th in Acadia International School and he dedicated this full book to a SST teacher ," Miss Shikha Mishra " .

In an interview conducted by NLP triquest , Suryansh Tripathi said ," My dream is to go into civil services. "

If you rate this book ; or review this book ; please call on   8077880769   or   email   us   at tripathi.suryanshkr2011@gmail.com.

Channels of Mr. Suryansh Tripathi

Instagram : its_hide45

Youtube : Suryansh pollux universe

MAKES A LOTS OF LOVE TO YOUR FUTURE AND ALSO THANKS A LOT FOR YOUR CORPORATION !

45